# RED RIDING HOOD

# RED RIDING HOOD

*Retold in verse for boys and girls to read themselves*

*by*

Beatrice Schenk de Regniers

*Drawings by Edward Gorey*

ALADDIN BOOKS

*Macmillan Publishing Company   New York*

*This one is for Mary*

*Aladdin Books*
*Macmillan Publishing Company*
*866 Third Avenue, New York, NY 10022*
*Collier Macmillan Canada, Inc.*
*First Aladdin Books edition 1977*
*Second Aladdin Books edition 1990*
*Printed in the United States of America*

*10   9   8   7   6   5   4   3   2   1*

*Library of Congress Cataloging-in-Publication Data*

*De Regniers, Beatrice Schenk.*
   *Red Riding Hood/retold in verse for boys and girls to read themselves by Beatrice Schenk de Regniers;*
*drawings by Edward Gorey. — 2nd Aladdin Books ed.*
        *p.        cm.*
   *Summary: Retells in verse the adventures of a little girl who meets a wolf in the forest on her way to visit*
*her grandmother.*

   *ISBN 0-689-71373-8*
   *[1. Stories in rhyme.   2. Fairy tales.   3. Folklore.]   I. Gorey, Edward, 1925-   ill.   II. Little Red*
*Riding Hood. English.   III. Title.*
*[PZ8.3.D443Re   1990]*
*398.21 — dc20*
*[E]        89-38024        CIP        AC*

# RED RIDING HOOD

Long ago
    There was a girl,
    Pretty and good.
    Her name was Little
    Red Riding Hood.

She wore
    A pretty red hood,
    A cape the same.
    And that's how Red Riding Hood
    Got her name.

One day
        Her mother told her,
        "I want you to take
        Your poor sick grandma
        This little cake.

        "You must go through the woods.
        I am going to worry."

        "Dear Mama," Red Riding Hood said,
        "I will hurry."

So

Red Riding Hood ran
For almost a mile.
Then she sat down
To rest a while.

Along came MR. WOLF!

He said,

      "Red Riding Hood!
      How nice to meet you.
      You look so pretty,
      I could eat you!

      I see your mama
      Was doing some baking.
      Tell me, Red Riding Hood,
      Where are you taking

               that little cake?"

Red Riding Hood said,
 "Oh, Mr. Wolf,
 I am going to take
 My poor sick grandma
 This little cake."

The wolf said,
 "And where does your grandma
 Live, my dear?"

 "Near the big oak tree.
 Not far from here,"
      Red Riding Hood said.

The wicked wolf thought,
 "Aha! Oho!
 I'll find a way
 To gobble two people
 Up today."

The wicked wolf said,
 "Red Riding Hood,
 Your grandma's sick.
 Don't you think
 That you should pick

     some flowers for her?"

"Oh, yes!" said Little
Riding Hood.
"I'm sure my poor sick
Grandma would
                    like some flowers."

She picked one flower,
And then another.
She quite forgot
She had promised her mother
                    to hurry.

But

The wolf ran fast—
Faster than fast.
He reached the grandma's
Door at last.

*Tap-tap!*

"Who is there? Who is there?"
Grandmama cried.

"Red Riding Hood.
Let me inside,"
              said the wolf.

He tried to make
His voice sound sweet.
"I've brought you a little
Cake to eat."

"Come in! Come in!"
Grandmama said.
"I can't get up.
I'm sick in bed."

*So the wolf opened the door and went inside and gobbled up the Grandmother.*

Then

      The wicked wolf
      Got into bed
      With Grandma's cap
      Upon his head.

                  He put on her glasses, too.

      And now he waits
      For you-know-who.
      And here she comes.
      What will she do?

She sees the door
Is open wide.
*Red Riding Hood!*
*Don't go inside!*

Red Riding Hood calls,
  "Grandma, Grandma!
  Are you there?
  Grandma, Grandma!
  Tell me where

          you are."

          But Grandma did not say a word.

Red Riding Hood ran
To her grandma's bed.
"Here is something for you
To eat," she said.

"See this little cake.
And here are some—Oh!
Grandma! Why do you
Look at me so?"

"Grandma, what big eyes you have."

"The better to see you, my dear."

"Grandma, what big arms you have!"

"The better to hug you, my dear."

"Oh, Grandma! What big teeth you have!"

**"The better to eat you!"**

And the wicked wolf,
Without more ado,
Ate Red Riding Hood
And the little cake, too.

Soon the wolf fell asleep.
He snored loud and long.
A hunter was passing.
He thought, "Something's wrong.

"I never have heard
The old lady snore
That loud and that long.
I'll just look in the door."

When the hunter saw the wolf,
he said,

    "So there you are,
    You mean old sinner!
    Have you eaten Red Riding Hood's
    Grandma for dinner?"

He took his knife
And he cut the wolf's belly.
Out jumped Red Riding Hood.
"Oh, it was smelly

in there," she said.

Then out came Grandma.

     "Thank goodness!" she cried.

     "What took you so long?

     I almost died

          in there."

The hunter said,
　　　"Now get lots of stones—
　　　Whatever it takes
　　　To fill the wolf's belly
　　　Before he awakes."

They put in the stones.
Then with needle and thread
Grandma sewed up the wolf
While he slept in her bed.

The wolf woke up.
He looked around.
He tried to run.
He fell to the ground.

           The stones were very heavy.

"This is the end,"
The wicked wolf said.
He took one more step
And he fell down dead.

           And that was the end of the wicked wolf.